QUERCUS THE OAK TREE

First paperback edition 2022

A series of books written by Neil Morton

Book design by Publishing Push

ILLUSTRATIONS by Zaria Mmanga

978-1-80227-591-9 (paperback)
978-1-80227-592-6 (ebook)

QUERCUS THE OAK TREE

A series of books written by Neil Morton

Illustrations by Zaria Mmanga

Like my brothers and sisters all over the world, I began life as a seed that grew on my Mother's branches.

My seed is called an acorn, and whilst I was growing, I sat in what can only be described as an egg cup, as you can see!

I can remember, all those years ago, looking down on the forest floor and thinking . . .

'What if I fell to the ground before autumn came, which is the time when all seeds fall to the ground?' I would probably be scorched by the hot summer sun or, even worse, eaten by a squirrel or wild pig!

This frightened me so much that I hung on to my Mother's branch as tight as I could. I did not want to fall too early in the year.

I knew how important it was for me to grow as big as possible, storing up food and energy in my shell so that when I did fall, I would have enough strength to push a root into the ground the following spring. That's when all trees start to grow.

COLOUR ME IN

As the summer of 1583 came to an end, the days became shorter and cooler. The winds started to blow. Sometimes it was so strong that it blew whole twigs to the ground with the acorns still attached.

'Please, Mother Nature, don't let this happen to me,' I thought. My chances of survival would not be good if that were to be the case.

That's what happened to my dear friend Tom.

"Oh no!" shouted Tom as he cartwheeled to the ground. "Now I am in trouble."

There was nothing I could do but watch in horror as my friend hit the ground with such force that he split his head open on the hard ground. Tom lay quite still, totally dazed and silent.

A few days later, I heard Tom's voice.

"Quercus, something funny has happened to me. I can feel something growing out of my shell; it looks like a root. Isn't it too early for this to happen?"

"Yes, Tom, I am afraid it is," I replied.

And that is when I knew he would not survive.

I knew that it was far too early to sprout a root, so I told him to be very brave and hope that some falling leaves would protect him from being burnt by Jack Frost because frosted tree roots result in certain death. A covering of leaves would hide him from those greedy squirrels or wild pigs. There was no fear of a forest pony eating him because acorns make ponies very ill.

I felt very sorry for Tom; he was such a nice friend. Sometimes life can be very cruel, cruel enough to make me even more determined to hang on until the right time to fall in the autumn, around November time. That's when all seeds fall to the ground.

Thousands of seeds fall to the ground every year, but only a few live to tell the tale. They need to fall in a place where they can feel the sun's heat and the gentle spring showers.

So, I had to wait for that north wind to blow. I had to land on the sunny, south side of my Mother and far enough away from the shade of her branches.

So I waited and waited for that north wind.

One day in November, the dark clouds of a storm appeared in the sky. All the big trees started to bend and shake with the force of the wind – but it was coming from the southwest!

"No!"' I shouted. "That's the wrong direction for me!" I knew it would mean I would land on the wrong side of my Mum and, worse still, in her shade.

Some trees can survive in conditions like these, but not me; I am what woodmen call a ' light demander.'

Suddenly, a great gush of wind hit my Mum and, *Whoosh*, I was flying through the air!

"Ouch!" I shouted. "That hurt."

"Are you alright, Quercus?" Tom asked feebly.

"Well, I have not cracked my head open like you, Tom."

Those were the last words I heard from Tom. He had become very weak in his efforts to push his root into the ground. He had no more strength to talk anymore.

I could not stay there for too long: a wild pig might eat me, and that thought terrified me.

Now I should explain that not only do seeds fall to the ground in the autumn, but leaves do too. Perhaps some might cover me up, or better still, a forest pony might step on me and push me into the ground. I would be safe then but sadly, not in the right place; I had to be in the sun, *somehow!*

I needed a bit of luck, and it came in an unexpected way.

Suddenly I heard someone shouting, "Left, right, left, right."

What on earth was coming my way? Then all of a sudden, I saw a band of soldiers marching towards me. The man at the back was obviously feeling tired because he was lurching from side to side. Just as he was passing, he tripped up and stepped on me. There I was, stuck to the mud on the bottom of his shoe and I remained there until they stopped for lunch.

I was now in the open where I needed to be, but not pushed into the ground.

AAAA!!!

After the soldiers had eaten their lunch, the man in charge shouted at my soldier and told him to clean up his shoes. That was the next bit of luck that came my way because he scraped me onto the ground using his dagger.

So there I was, lying in a pool of mud, waiting for someone to step on me one more time. By sheer chance, my soldier did, bless him. My life as a tree was about to begin.

I fell asleep knowing that if Nature was kind to me, I would grow a root in the spring and from that root a leaf stem. Life, however, is not that simple for a young oak tree, or any other tree for that matter, as you will find out in Book 2!

Would you like to grow your own oak tree? Well turn the page over and read the instructions telling you how to do it. How cool is that!!

THINGS YOU MIGHT LIKE TO DO NEXT AUTUMN

How about growing your own oak tree? How cool would that be?

How many butterflies can you count throughout the book?

HERE'S HOW YOU DO IT

1. Find a mature oak tree (over 50 years old) in the autumn when the acorns are falling to the ground. Remember oak trees only produce acorns every four years, sometimes up to seven year intervals may apply so you might have to search for some time, but they are there somewhere!

2. Collect the acorns, put them in a bag. When you get home, fill a bucket with water and throw them in. The acorns that float are no good, so throw them away. Take the ones that have sunk and discard the really dark brown ones. The best acorns are a nice light brown or not too green.

3. Get a 6" plastic flower pot and fill it with a peat free compost. Best to mix in some sand or sawdust. Fill the pot to within 2 cms from the top. Then make four holes around the edge with your finger and put an acorn in each one **POINTED**

END UP – most important. Cover acorns with 2 cms of compost and place pot outside. To protect them from birds or squirrels, cover the top with chicken netting or something similar.

4. Keep the pots watered and in the spring, you will see a shoot appear and then you will be the proud owner of your own oak tree.

   Look up on Google '**Plants for kids-oak**' and it will tell you how to look after your young oak tree for the first few years.

> You can buy acorns on the internet, click onto
> **Plant World seeds Quercus robur (oak tree) acorns.**
>
> If you store acorns make sure they are put in a dark cool place like a garage. If you have collected them sow within **2 weeks.**

One day we could all get together and plant our trees to create a new wood!

How cool would that be and then you could say you have done your little bit to save this wonderful planet of ours and your trees will be around for hundreds of years, just like **Quercus**.

Lightning Source UK Ltd.
Milton Keynes UK
UKRC030250161222
413979UK00001B/9